This book is loosely based on an actual event: Charles I's escape from imprisonment at Hampton Court Palace in 1647, during the Civil War. To find out more about the truth behind this tale, please visit:

www.hrp.org.uk

First published 2015 by Walker Books Ltd, 87 Vauxhall Walk, London SE11 5HJ
in association with Historic Royal Palaces, Hampton Court Palace, Surrey KT8 9AU

10 9 8 7 6 5 4 3 2 1

© 2015 Historic Royal Palaces & Walker Books Ltd

This book has been typeset in Garamond

Printed in China

British Library Cataloguing in Publication Data: a catalogue record for this book is available from the British Library

ISBN 978-1-4063-6606-8 (hb)
ISBN 978-1-4063-6607-5 (pb)

www.walker.co.uk

REX
AND THE
ROYAL PRISONER

Illustrated by Kate Sheppard

WALKER BOOKS
AND SUBSIDIARIES
LONDON · BOSTON · SYDNEY · AUCKLAND

Historic
Royal Palaces

Rex was hungry. He'd been chasing the ravens all day, and it was hours until dinner time. He decided to sniff out some food.

He jumped into his favourite bin and began to dig.
It was dirty and stinky and overflowing with rubbish.
Just the way I like it, thought Rex, as he
burrowed deeper and deeper.

Before he knew it,
he was falling.

He tumbled and turned
and twisted around

and landed with a

THUD !

Rex wobbled to his feet, shook a chocolate wrapper from his head and looked around. Where am I? he wondered. Red-brick turrets rose up above a yawning gateway. This wasn't the Tower of London! Just then, he caught a whiff of something meaty and delicious. He decided to follow the smell.

The delicious smell led him to the most enormous kitchens filled with pies, puddings and strings of sausages. A huge piece of meat was cooking above the fireplace. Rex reached up to take a bite.

"Watch out!" said a voice. "The cook hit me with a frying pan once."

Rex turned to see a sad-looking spaniel curled up on the floor.

"I'm Rogue," said the spaniel. "Are you new to Hampton Court Palace?"

So *that's* where I am, thought Rex. "Yes. I'm Rex."

"Shh!" hissed Rogue. "'Rex' means 'king'. And kings aren't popular at the moment."

"Why not?" asked Rex.

"Haven't you heard?" said Rogue. "My master, King Charles I, has been taken prisoner – Oliver Cromwell says he can't be king any more. He's locked up in the palace, but there are 1,500 rooms…"

"I'll help you find him," said Rex. "We just need to follow his scent."

They tracked the
King's scent around
the Great Hall …

… and through the Haunted Gallery.
"Is it really haunted?" Rex asked nervously.
"No time to find out!"
barked Rogue.
"We need to find
my master!"

But when they reached the Chapel Royal, they lost the scent.
"It's hopeless," whimpered Rogue. "We'll never find him."
Then she sniffed the air… "He went this way!" she barked,
and they raced out into the gardens.

The scent led them to a room with a small window. Rex and Rogue jumped up to look inside. There, at a writing desk, was a thin man with a neat moustache.
"The King!" cried Rogue. "We have to get in!" But the door was locked…

They barked and howled till a man came to see what the fuss was about.
"It's Mr Herbert, my master's servant," said Rogue.

Mr Herbert opened the door. "Hello, Rogue," he said. "Come in, while no one's looking…"

"Rogue!" cried the King. "And you've brought a friend!
Didn't the guards stop you?"
"The guards are on their tea break, Your Majesty," said Mr Herbert.
A slow smile spread across the King's face.
"Herbert, why don't you take a break, too," he said.
"Very good, Your Majesty," said Mr Herbert.

As soon as Mr Herbert had left the room, the King clapped
his hands with glee.
"This is my chance to escape!" he cried. "Quick, Rogue –
before the guards come back."
The King slipped out of the door. Rogue scampered behind.
"I'll stay here to throw the guards off the track…" barked Rex.

A few minutes later, there was a rat-tat-tat at the door. "I've come to take the King to chapel," said a guard. There was no reply. "Are you in there?" called the guard. "I'll give you 10 seconds. 1 … 2 … 3 …" The King needed more time to get away. How could Rex trick the guard?

Rat-
tat-
tat!

He jumped onto the chair and hid himself under the King's cloak and hat.

"8 … 9 … 10!"
The guard peered
through the keyhole.
"I'm tired of waiting.
Chapel's nearly over!"
he growled.
Rex growled back…
"Hold on," said the guard.
"You're not the King,"
and he burst into
the room.

"Help! Help! The King has escaped!" cried the guard,
as he ran into the garden. Rex was hot on his heels.

"Stop!" barked Rex,
as he jumped on the
guard's back.
"Got you!" barked
Rogue as she bit
the guard's ankle.
"Get off!" cried the
guard, as he reached
out to grab the King.

But the King pushed the guard into the river.

"We did it!" barked Rex, and they leaped onto the boat.

They rowed down the river and stopped by a field where
a horse was grazing. As they stepped ashore, the King removed
his beautiful pearl earring.
"This is for you, Rex," he said. "I'll never forget what you've done for me."
Rex wagged his tail as the King slipped the earring onto his collar.

Then the King scooped up Rogue and jumped onto the horse.
"To the Isle of Wight!" he cried.
"Thank you for helping my master," barked Rogue. "Won't you come with us?"
But Rex's nose had begun to twitch. "I have to go home," he said.

Rex could smell something stinky, something juicy, something extremely delicious. It was his litter bin.

He jumped in
and dug down deep,
till he felt himself falling.

He tumbled and turned
and twisted around,
and landed
with a

THUD!

He was back home at the Tower of London. He heard
a familiar voice. "Rex! Dinner time!"

The next day, Rex noticed a painting he'd never seen before – a portrait of King Charles I, with two dogs at his feet. One was Rogue … and he recognized the other dog, too. A very scruffy dog who looked an awful lot like him, with something on his collar … a pearl earring.